D0190378

For Ellie and Douglas
V. C.

First published 2014 by Walker Books Ltd
87 Vauxhall Walk, London SE11 5HJ

This edition published 2014

2 4 6 8 10 9 7 5 3 1

Text © 2014 Jeanne Willis
Illustrations © 2014 Vanessa Cabban

The right of Jeanne Willis and Vanessa Cabban to be identified
as author and illustrator respectively of this work has been asserted
by them in accordance with the Copyright, Designs and Patents Act 1988

This book has been typeset in Cochin

Printed in China

British Library Cataloguing in Publication Data:
a catalogue record for this book
is available from the British Library

ISBN 978-1-4063-3292-6

www.walker.co.uk

WALKER BOOKS
AND SUBSIDIARIES
LONDON · BOSTON · SYDNEY · AUCKLAND

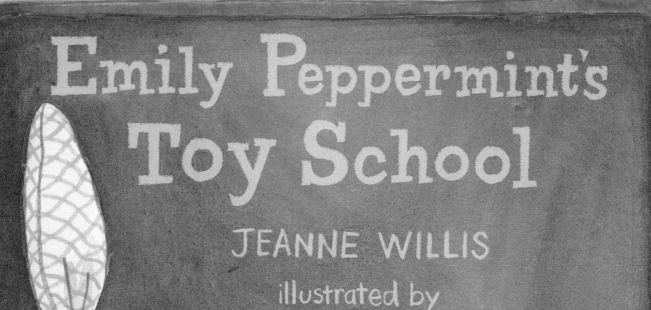

Emily Peppermint's Toy School

JEANNE WILLIS

illustrated by

VANESSA CABBAN

"Welcome to Toy School everybody!"
said Emily Peppermint. "Who can tell me what
we'll be learning today?
Hands up."

"I haven't got any hands!" said Shmoo.

"Miss? Miss! Are we going to learn how to do our hair like a princess?" asked Edie.

"I haven't got any hair!" said Tinny Tim.

"The reason you are here is to learn all about children," said Emily. "Because one day, you will belong to a child."

"What is a child?"
asked Gumbo. "Do they
have four legs, little horns
and long necks?"

"Do they growl
when you tip them
upside down?"
said Little Ted.

"No two children are alike," explained Emily. "But they all begin as babies."

"That one's pinned together," said Little Ted.

"That's a nappy," said Emily. "Babies wet themselves."

"I wish I could wet myself," said Edie.

"Plastic dolls can. Are babies made of plastic?"

"Babies aren't made like toys,"
explained Emily.
"They're born and grow
into children."

"Grow?" gasped Edie. "If I grew,
my knickers wouldn't fit!"
"You forgot to put them on,"
said Gumbo.

Just then Rose, who helped Emily
in the classroom, came in pushing
an enormous pram.

"Park the pram on the rug, please," said Emily. "Then the toys won't get hurt when I teach them how to fall out of it."

Rose handed out the safety helmets.

"Miss, why do we have to wear funny hats?" asked Little Ted.

"If you gather round, I'll explain," said Emily.

"If you belong to a baby, you might
get thrown out of the pram."

"Aghhh!" panicked Shmoo.
"I don't want to belong to
a baby. Babies are bad!"
"Babies aren't bad,"
said Emily. "Remember our
school motto: **Good toys
make good children.**

"When a baby throws you
about, it's just being playful.
As a good toy, you just
have to play along.

"Rose will now demonstrate the correct way to land."

One by one, the class practised falling out of the pram.

"Gumbo, keep those knees tucked in," said Emily.

"I can do roly-polies,"
 said Shmoo.
"Wheee…!"
"Duck!" called Emily.
"Who me?" said Rose.
"No, look out!" said Emily.

"Now, let's go outside
and practise without
the rug," said Emily.

"It's a lovely day for being
thrown out of a pram,
isn't it?" said Rose.

Everyone followed Emily
onto the field.

"Climb in, Class," said Emily.
"When I call your name, fling
yourself out as if you'd been
thrown by a great big baby."

"Off we go…"

"Tinny Tim...
Jump!"

But as Tinny Tim fell,
his clockwork key knocked
the brake ...

and the pram began
to roll down the hill …

with all
the toys inside it…

"Oh no!" shouted Emily.
"Run, Rose!"

"I've got a stitch," said Rose.
"Several stitches actually.
My side seam has come undone."

"Peepers porkers!" gasped Emily. "They're heading
for a muddy ditch!"
But just as she had almost caught the pram handle,
it hit a rock and …

... all the toys
flew out.

SPLAT!

"Don't worry, Miss!" said Gumbo. "We landed perfectly."

"I've got a screw loose," bleeped Tinny Tim.

"That's nothing new," said Edie.

Back in the classroom, Emily Peppermint announced
the next lesson. "Children need clean toys," said Emily.
"This afternoon, I'm going to teach you
how to swim …

"… in the washing-up bowl.

Who wants to go first?"

Rosemary Moon's
ice cream
machine book

Rosemary Moon's
ice cream
machine book

*Frozen delights to prepare —
home-made ice creams, sherbets, sorbets,
frozen yoghurts, and desserts*

APPLE

This book is for Kate Bishop, who won an
ice-cream machine and has never looked back since.

A QUINTET BOOK

Published by Apple Press
Sheridan House
112-116A Western Road
Hove
East Sussex BN3 1DD

ISBN 1-84092-317-2

Reprinted in 2000, 2001, 2002

This book was designed and produced by
Quintet Publishing Limited
6 Blundell Street
London N7 9BH

Creative Director: Richard Dewing
Art Director: Silke Braun
Design: Balley Design Associates
Simon Balley & Joanna Hill
Project Editor: Diana Steedman
Editor: Lisa Cussans
Photographer: Andrew Sydenham
Food Stylist: Jennie Berresford

Typeset in Great Britain by Central Southern Typesetters, Eastbourne
Manufactured in Singapore by Eray Scan Pte Ltd
Printed in Singapore by Star Standard Industries (Pte) Ltd

The recipes in this book have been compiled for
use in a variety of ice cream machines, or indeed without a machine at all.
Always refer to your manufacturer's instructions regarding capacity and operation.

CONTENTS

Introduction

Making ice cream at home must be one of the most creative and utterly indulgent forms of cooking there is. In the old days, ice-cream making was a bore, since it was necessary to take the mixture out of the freezer two, three or more times during the freezing process in order to beat it vigorously, an essential labour to ensure the finished confection was not full of ice crystals.

Nowadays, ice-cream making couldn't be easier, following the advent of the domestic ice-cream machine. These come in all shapes and sizes, bearing a startling range of price tags, but all transform the actual freezing and mixing, or churning, of ice creams into a quick and simple job. This book shows how to make a selection of ice creams, sorbets and other frozen desserts with the minimum of fuss and effort, using an ice-cream machine to do the tedious work. Take away the effort, and preparing ice creams is almost as much fun as eating them!

An Internationally Popular Food

Ice cream is one of the world's most popular foods. It is a firm favourite with children, and a sophisticated, seductive and satisfying confection for the rest of us. If there are Seven Ages of Man, then ice cream is pretty much a perfect food for all of them.

The international perception of ice cream has changed dramatically during the last decade of the 20th century. The discerning shopper wants to buy products made from "real" ingredients, so there has been a tremendous move towards "old-fashioned" ice creams made with milk or cream, eggs and pure flavourings. The designer commercial ice creams now available are exceptional in flavour and texture but, more than ever before, you get what you pay for. The luxury product comes with luxury price tag.

Making ice cream at home is not an economical process. I believe there is no point in embarking on the preparation of an ice cream if you are not going to produce an even better result than the best products available in the shops. To do this you must use the best ingredients: the freshest eggs and cream or milk, ripe, unblemished fruits, quality flavourings and the finest chocolate, coffee and nuts.

This book is about luxury and indulgence, but it also has a conscience, and so includes a delicious selection of recipes for reduced-fat ice creams and ices. Whether you are addicted to rich ice creams, Italian gelatos, sorbets or ice milks, you will find recipes here to tempt and titillate. I hope you will discover not only new ideas for flavours, but also styles of ice creams and ices you may not have tried before—lightly creamy sherbets and wonderful frozen yogurts. I hope that you enjoy them all as much as I have.